KIDS CAN'T STOP READING
THE CHOOSE YOUR
OWN ADVENTURE® STORIES

"Choose Your Own Adventure _____ _____
that has come along _____ _____ _____
_____ ____ age 11

"I didn't read much ___ ___ ____ I read my
Choose Your Own _____ books almost
every night."

—Chris Brogan, age 13

"I love the control I have over what happens
next."

—Kosta Efstathiou, age 17

"Choose Your Own Adventure books are so
much fun to read and collect—I want them all!"
—Brendan Davin, age 11

And teachers like this series, too:

"We have read and reread, worn thin, loved,
loaned, bought for others, and donated to school
libraries our Choose Your Own Adventure
books."

CHOOSE YOUR OWN ADVENTURE®—
AND MAKE READING MORE FUN!

Bantam Books in the Choose Your Own Adventure® series
Ask your bookseller for the books you have missed

THE REALITY MACHINE

BY EDWARD PACKARD

ILLUSTRATED BY JUNE BRIGMAN

BANTAM BOOKS
NEW YORK · TORONTO · LONDON · SYDNEY · AUCKLAND

RL 4, age 10 and up

THE REALITY MACHINE

A Bantam Book/December 1993

*CHOOSE YOUR OWN ADVENTURE® is a registered
trademark of Bantam Books,
a division of Bantam Doubleday Dell Publishing Group, Inc.
Registered in U.S. Patent and Trademark Office and elsewhere.*

Original conception of Edward Packard

*Cover art by Catherine Huerta
Interior illustrations by June Brigman*

ISBN 0-553-56401-3

Published simultaneously in the United States and Canada

*Bantam Books are published by Bantam Books, a division of
Bantam Doubleday Dell Publishing Group, Inc. Its trademark,
consisting of the words "Bantam Books" and the portrayal of a
rooster, is Registered in U.S. Patent and Trademark Office and
in other countries. Marca Registrada. Bantam Books, 1540
Broadway, New York, New York 10036.*

PRINTED IN THE UNITED STATES OF AMERICA

OPM   0 9 8 7 6 5 4 3 2

THE REALITY
MACHINE

REALITY UNLIMITED, INC.

surreal action games

(999) 555–9599

Dr. Nicholas Telos, Ph.D.
President

WARNING!!!

Do not read this book straight through from beginning to end. These pages contain many different adventures you may have when you try out a super-advanced virtual reality machine.

From time to time as you read along, you'll have a chance to make a choice. What happens will be determined by your choices. You are responsible because you choose. After making your decision, follow the instructions to find out what happens next.

Think carefully. Sharp hand-eye coordination won't be enough when you play the Reality Machine. But if you're brave, alert, and clever, you'll have some of the most challenging and intense experiences of your life.

Good luck!

You never spent much time at the video arcade until SURREAL ACTION came along. SURREAL is one of the new virtual reality games. You don't just work knobs and a stick, you wear special goggles and gloves. You don't just look at a screen: everything you see is part of the game. And when you move your hands, you see them right in the action.

If you're out in space, clinging to the side of a spacecraft, you see your hands move just as you would if you were the astronaut. If you're trying to hook up a cosmic ray monitor, you see your fingers trying to attach a hook. A latch springs open, striking your fingers. But you don't just watch it—you really *feel* it. And if you flinch and lose your grip on the hook, you'll see the monitor fly off into space.

This sort of thing, and a lot more, happens when you're playing SURREAL ACTION. Your spacecraft is trying to land on Mars. It spins out. You wrestle with the stick to control it, your hands trembling with the vibration. A buzzer sounds behind your shoulder. You look around and see a red light on the pressure gauge. You snap on your oxygen mask and punch in the fault-search code. You've got to have quick hands—this is no kiddy game. When it's over, and you slip off your goggles and gloves, you feel as if you've returned from another world.

Turn to page 2.

As far as you're concerned, there's no game more fun than SURREAL ACTION. You play it every chance you get. And you're good at it—better than anyone you know. There's only one trouble: SURREAL ACTION is expensive. If you don't stop playing it so much, you're going to go broke!

One Saturday you're playing SURREAL ACTION and concentrating really hard, trying to make your money last. In this version of the game you're microscopic. You're on a kitchen table and a giant saltshaker towers over you. A bread crumb looks like a small hill. You can touch the huge white crystals of salt, big as boulders, scattered about you. You don't have much time to explore, however. A cone-headed dust mite, which looks about ten feet high to you, is coming at you. It has jaws that would frighten a shark.

You duck its attack and try to throw it off balance with a quick shove of your hand. You can just imagine how its heavy, bristly, slightly sticky abdomen feels as your hand brushes against it. With a terrific shove you manage to tip it over, but another one is already coming at you, and then another!

You keep the game going almost twenty minutes, fighting off two, then three, then four, and finally as many as a dozen cone-headed dust mites. But there's no way to win this game. You're finally done in by an even bigger creature —a killer ant. Game over.

Go on to the next page.

4

You slip off your goggles and gloves. Your face is covered with sweat. You keep looking around, expecting another attack. But instead of dust mites there are only normal-sized people in the arcade.

"Hey—that was some battle." A man's voice brings you back to reality—the other reality.

"You've got great talent," the man says when you glance around at him. "You're the best SUR-REAL ACTION player I've ever seen."

"Thanks." You like the compliment, but you wonder who this guy is. He has a mustache and carefully groomed hair and is wearing a gray suit and striped tie—he looks like a respectable businessman. What's he hanging around arcades for?

Sensing your suspicions, he hands you his business card.

You look up from reading it. "Your company makes this game?" you ask.

He flashes a proud smile. "Right here in this town."

"It's a neat game."

"Well, thank you—we think so too," he says. "And we're working on much better ones."

"I can't wait to try them," you say.

Go on to the next page.

"How would you like to make some money next Saturday?" he asks. "We've been developing a fabulous new product. I'm looking for someone to test it out. Maybe you'd be interested. We pay ten dollars an hour—you'll have trouble beating that!"

"Sounds great," you say.

Dr. Telos gives you the company's address. You agree to be there the following Saturday morning.

Your parents are amazed when you tell them about your conversation with Dr. Telos. "I never knew playing arcade games could be anything but a waste of money," your dad says. "It's nice to know you can get back some of what you've been spending."

Turn to page 23.

6

"I'll tell you," he says. "Merc and I didn't move the whole time. You were watching a holographic videotape of us. The tape was played in slow motion. The illusion works because the brain tries to make sense of what it sees and hears."

"But—"

"There's more to it than that, of course," Telos adds. "It's highly technical—I'm afraid you'd have to be a scientist to understand it."

"I believe it," you say. "Wow, I just can't get over it—the feeling of being able to go faster than anything else."

"Imagine taking this game to a higher level," Dr. Telos says.

"It's hard to imagine," you say.

In a lower voice he says, "With what we're working on now, it won't be just a *feeling* you're having. It will be what I call TIME REALITY. That's level two of the game."

"You mean I'd actually be able to run faster than a dog?"

Go on to the next page.

"At level two—yes." He picks up a dish of chips in each hand and holds them in front of you. "These green-striped chips speed up your bodily processes, the red-striped chips slow them down. If you chose to speed up the processes, then your thoughts and body movements will all happen much faster. You'll be able to run at superhuman speed, not just imagine it. As I said, these chips have already been programmed by the Reality Machine. You won't even have to be connected. I'll just affix a chip behind your ear."

"Whoa—hold on a moment," you say.

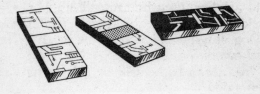

Turn to page 26.

8

Late that afternoon you do what you've been itching to do all day. First, you check the world record for the hundred-meter dash in your copy of the *Guinness Book of Records;* then you bike over to the high school track. It's begun to drizzle, and there's no one around. You stand at the starting line and glance at the sweep hand of your watch. When it finally reaches the 12 at the top, you take off.

You know right away you're fast—you can feel the ground flying by beneath your feet. But you have to slow down a little for the last hundred feet or so—you're not in shape to sprint the distance. When you cross the line and check your watch, you let out a little yell: you just ran the hundred-meter dash in eight and half seconds, beating the world record!

Turn to page 31.

"This has to do with a game we're designing for SURREAL ACTION II," he says. "It's called HURRICANE. When you're wearing the new goggles we've developed, that ship won't look like a toy. It will look like a real ship on a real ocean. And we've recently made a breakthrough on sense generators that can make you really feel wet and cold, as if waves were pouring over the rail. Technology has improved greatly since SURREAL ACTION. We want people to be able to truly *feel* the action as well as see it, all with electronic impulses!"

You're impressed, but you're also curious. "So what exactly do you have in mind for me, Dr. Telos?"

"Something even more advanced than this," he says. "Come with me into the lab—I'll show you." He leads you down the hall and into a large, windowless room. The floor is covered with a pale green carpet. Cameras, spotlights, and audio speakers are mounted on the ceiling and walls. Near the entrance is a file cabinet and a small desk. On the desk are a portable computer and a telephone. In the middle of the room stands a cube-shaped booth with Plexiglas walls on three sides. Inside the booth is a leather chair, computers, and other equipment. A helmet and an oversize pair of gloves are connected to the chair by electric cables.

Go on to the next page.

You walk over to the booth. "This doesn't look anything like SURREAL ACTION," you say.

"SURREAL ACTION is tiddlywinks compared to this," Dr. Telos says. "This is called the Reality Machine. I'll show you some of the things we can do with it."

Turn to page 27.

The following Saturday when you arrive at the offices of Reality Unlimited, the door is unlocked, but no one is around. You go through the reception room to the lab and find Dr. Telos there, jogging around the room. You call to him, but he pays no attention.

He must be wearing a chip from the Reality Machine, you think. You watch him for a moment and notice that he's following a square rather than a circular path. Each time he comes back to where he started he slaps the air as if he's giving someone a high five. He repeats this motion, then stops and bends forward.

You call to him again. Still no answer. He makes fists with his hands and holds them together, one over the other. His feet are planted at right angles to you, but his head is turned toward you.

"Dr. Telos, it's me," you call. Though his eyes are fixed on you, it's obvious he doesn't recognize you. By now you're convinced that he's gone insane. You pick up the telephone and dial 911. An operator says he'll send a couple of men over immediately.

Turn to page 112.

"I'll try it," you say. "It might be fun."

"Good." Dr. Telos takes the adhesive off a green-striped chip and presses the chip onto the skin behind your ear. "That's all there is to it," he says. "Feel okay?"

"Not bad," you say, though there's a kind of fuzzy sensation around your head, as if your hair were standing on end. Otherwise, you can't complain.

"Now . . . watch . . . me," Telos says slowly. He picks up the ball again—it seems to take him several seconds to do so. Meanwhile, Merc, also in slow motion, is getting to his feet.

"See . . . if . . . you . . . can . . . beat . . . Merc . . . to . . . the . . . ball," Dr. Telos says. Again it seems as if he's talking and throwing the ball in slow motion. And Merc runs after it in slow motion. You take off after him at regular speed. Once again you seem to run faster than the greyhound! After you pick up the ball, you remove the chip from behind your ear.

"Just like level one, right?" Dr. Telos says, talking at normal speed. "But this time it was real. You really *did* run faster than Merc. Because your bodily processes were speeded up!"

"I'd sure like to try this out playing sports," you say.

Turn to page 30.

"These electronic chips were programmed in the Reality Machine for SUPER TIME—level two," Dr. Telos says. Then he takes out a third dish, this one containing several black chips. "And these are for level two of SUPER SPACE. The chips for both games are coated with a special adhesive on one side and can be worn unobtrusively behind the ear."

"What do you mean 'unobtrusively'?"

"I mean in a way that people won't notice—out of sight behind your ear."

"What do the chips do?"

"That's the most fantastic part of all." Telos picks up several of the striped chips and holds them out in his palm. "These chips for SUPER TIME affect the pace of your body movements." He puts them back in the dish and picks up some of the black chips. "And these, for SUPER SPACE, affect your perceptions of space around you and everything in it, including your own body! In each case the chips, when affixed behind the ear, interact with the electrical activity in the brain. They create effects that almost defy belief."

You pick up one of the chips and look at it.

Turn to page 88.

"I'm not sure I want to go through with this if bad things are going to happen," you say.

"Don't misunderstand me," Dr. Telos says. "I think you're going to enjoy this a lot. But of course there will be challenges—that's part of what makes it fun. I just wanted to make sure you didn't panic in situations that look critical and seem awfully real."

"I guess that should be no problem," you say. Still, you feel your heart beating faster.

"Okay then, ready?"

"Ready."

Suddenly all goes black. A moment later there's plenty of light. You're in the cockpit of a spacecraft, sitting on the end of a runway.

A voice sounds in your headphones. "Ready for launch, Commander?"

You can't believe how real this seems—you have to remind yourself it's only a simulation, like some fantastic hologram.

"Commander, do you read us?"

"Oh, yes . . . ready."

An amber light blinks on your instrument panel. The voice says, "Ready for countdown?"

"Yes," you answer in a trembling voice.

"Manual or auto control for launch?"

"Auto control," you answer. You don't feel quite ready for manual.

Turn to page 85.

"I'll play SUPER TIME," you say. "But I still don't get how this works."

"It's a simple enough concept," Dr. Telos says. "Just as SUPER SPACE creates artificial space, SUPER TIME creates artificial time."

"How can it do that?"

"The basic idea is that you'll have a sensation of time slowing down—or speeding up. Imagine the power you'd have if everything but yourself moved more slowly. I mean *everything*—even the hands of a clock! Or, if everything moved much more swiftly than you—it would be like fast-forwarding into the future, living hundreds of years from now and still being young!"

"These ideas are making my head spin."

"That's part of what our business is about," Dr. Telos says. "I wish I could explain things more fully, but you really have to experience these projects to understand them."

You think about this a moment, then say, "Dr. Telos, you don't actually mean you can *affect* time, do you? Don't you mean you can affect how time *seems* to pass?"

He gives you a sly wink. "Judge for yourself. That's part of your job." He picks up the phone. "Send Merc in," he says. "That's my dog," he explains. "A two-year-old greyhound."

A moment later the door opens. Jason appears, with a sleek-looking hound straining at his leash. Jason lets the dog loose. It rushes up to Dr. Telos and nuzzles his hand.

Turn to page 50.

18

Suddenly you realize that you're supposed to be racing him. You break into a run. Unlike the ball and the dog, you run flat out at high speed. You watch the ball drifting down, touching the rug, beginning to roll. Running at full speed toward it is Merc. You quickly pass him, reach down, and scoop up the ball with one hand. You glance back at Merc, who is slowly putting on the brakes, a surprised look on his face.

Amazed, you pull off the helmet. The dog, back at regular speed, jumps for the ball in your hand. You toss it lightly aside. It travels at regular speed. So does Merc, who snatches it in an instant. Dr. Telos is laughing.

"Wow, that was something," you say. "Was I really running faster than a greyhound?"

"No," the scientist says, his face turning serious. "It was just an illusion—but a pretty good one, don't you think?"

"Yeah, sensational. I don't see how you did it!"

Turn to page 6.

You decide this is your best chance to escape. You get to your feet and start hopping toward the entrance. You look over your shoulder and see Wolfie's head turning slowly toward you. A look of alarm gradually spreads over his face. Slowly his hand moves toward his gun.

"Stop!" he yells. But by then you've hopped out of the room. Another second, and you're through the back door and onto the driveway. He chases you, but he can't catch up.

You round the back of the house, panting for breath—hopping is harder than you'd realized. You've almost reached the street when you look over your shoulder and see that Wolfie has rounded the corner too and is slowly aiming the gun at you, his finger squeezing the trigger. A bullet is heading for you!

Though the bullet seems slowed down, it's still coming at terrific speed. You duck just in time.

Wolfie is crouching, aiming. He fires again. Another bullet's coming. You twist sideways. The bullet only grazes your sleeve. But still another comes. You twist wildly and escape it but lose your balance. The next bullet cuts through your jeans, nicking your thigh.

Wolfie stops shooting—he's out of ammunition. Your thigh hurts, but you can still hop, so you keep moving—out into the road. A pickup truck is coming. The driver brakes. He's about to hit you, but with your lightning speed, you hop past the front bumper.

Turn to page 48.

"Herb, where's that ambulance?" one of the cops asks the other.

"It may not be necessary," you say. You run up to Dr. Telos, but the way he keeps moving, you can't get close to him.

He stands at the imaginary plate, lightly swinging his imaginary bat, squinting in imaginary sunlight at the imaginary pitcher about to throw a ball. Once again he rotates his arms as if swinging at a ball. Then he's still for a moment, waiting for the pitch.

You quickly reach up and rip the black chip off from behind his ear.

Dr. Telos looks dazedly around. "What's going on?"

"You were playing SUPER BASEBALL," you say. "You must have forgotten you could take off the chip."

"Yes, that's true—something must have gone wrong with the program." He hurries over to the Reality Machine, then turns abruptly away from it.

"You okay now?" one of the cops asks.

Dr. Telos slowly nods his head. "What I've been through! It was great hitting those home runs, but the way I couldn't stop—that was awful."

"I'm sure glad you came out of it," you say.

He nods. "Me too. And I haven't even tried SUPER TIME yet."

The End

At 10:00 A.M. that Saturday you show up at the offices of Reality Unlimited. A young man in a white coat is seated at the reception desk.

"I'm Jason Traynor, Dr. Telos's assistant," he says when you introduce yourself. "Dr. Telos is expecting you."

A few minutes later Dr. Telos, this time dressed in a white lab coat, comes out to greet you.

"Glad you're here," he says. "All set to go to work?"

"Sure thing," you say.

"Good. Well then, before we start, I'll show you where special effects are created for SURREAL ACTION." He leads you into what could be a prop room for a film producer. A model of a spaceship is suspended by thin wire. Behind it is an illuminated screen filled with stars, planets, and nebulae. Nearby is a tank in which tiny waves are being whipped up by a fan. Dr. Telos points to a toy boat, held by an almost invisible thread, riding the waves, pitching and rolling as if it were a real ship in a storm.

Turn to page 10.

Jason, pale with fear, starts to obey. You freeze, afraid that any movement will show you're speeded up.

Meanwhile, Wolfie, who also seems slowed down, motions with his gun for you to follow Jason.

Wolfie hasn't put his chip on yet. With your terrific speed, you might be able to knock the gun out of his hand before he reacts. You're fast, but suppose you're not fast enough. If only you could get Jason to distract him!

If you try to use your speed to knock Wolfie's gun out of his hand, turn to page 77.

If you try to think of a way to get Jason to distract him, turn to page 82.

Another second and the ball is free, spinning as it slowly floats through the air. By the time it's a foot or so from the end of Dr. Telos's fingers, Merc's forepaws are off the ground. You watch them stretch out in front of him. First one rear leg and then the other leaves the ground. Soon his whole body is stretched out, his legs slowly coiling, springing, touching down—beginning to run in slow motion. The ball, though it too is moving in slow motion, is traveling much faster. It's already fifteen feet in front of the dog.

You watch, fascinated. You can see the ball slackening slightly, traveling in a curve that brings it closer to the floor. Merc begins to gain on it.

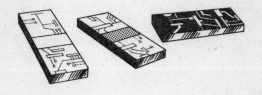

Turn to page 18.

Dr. Telos puts the dishes back on the table. "Of course, you don't have to try it if you don't want to," he says. "And if you do try it, and you don't like the experience you're having, you can just reach up and pull the chip off."

It's hard to believe Dr. Telos would ask you to try something that wasn't safe. And TIME REALITY sounds like the experience of a lifetime. On the other hand you're not so sure . . .

*If you decide to try out a chip,
turn to page 14.*

*If you decide against it,
turn to page 40.*

Dr. Telos steps into the booth and rests a hand on the back of the chair. "Everything is measured in space or time, so we've developed two games for the Reality Machine," he says. "One is called SUPER TIME and the other is called SUPER SPACE. We want to see how these games would work when played by typical customers. So your job will be simply to try them out. Choose the game you want to try first. You'll begin at level one, and then later you'll get a chance to try level two."

"What's the difference between level one and level two?"

"You can see best by trying them out," he replies. "But essentially, level one is like SURREAL ACTION and HURRICANE, only more advanced. You wear a special helmet and gloves, which contain software programmed by the Reality Machine. Events will seem to actually happen, including those you cause yourself—I promise you'll be astonished by how real they seem."

"Sounds fantastic," you say. "And level two does even more than that?"

Dr. Telos reaches into the cabinet, takes out two small glass dishes, and sets them on the table. Each dish contains several dull gray chips about three-quarters of an inch long. The chips in one dish have a thin band of green across the middle, the chips in the other dish a thin band of red.

Turn to page 15.

Wolfie ignores you. Slowly he gets into the car. The engine roars. The car starts to pull away. You sit up, aim for the back tire, and pull the trigger. Your bullet bounces off the bumper. You fire again, cutting a hole through the left fender. You pull the trigger again and don't even hit the car. You aim again and hit the trunk.

The car stops. Why? What's Wolfie doing? You take aim on the tire. With the car stopped, you should have no trouble hitting it this time, but you hesitate, trying to figure out his game.

*If you shoot out the tire,
turn to page 63.*

*If you wait to see what Wolfie does next,
turn to page 64.*

"Good. And I'd like you to see how this works outside the lab. That's the *real* test of the Reality Machine. But I think that's enough lab work for today," Dr. Telos continues. "Come back next Saturday, and we'll take it from there. Meanwhile, do you want to put the green-striped chip back on? We'll pay for every hour you wear it, even if you're home."

"Sounds okay to me," you say.

"Just remember when you get out on the street that everything is happening slowly. On the other hand, people will see *you* moving at four times the speed you're feeling. So you want to start practicing doing everything in slow motion—talking, walking, moving your arms, everything. Show off your speed only at certain times. Mostly take it real slow."

"Sounds hard to remember," you say, "but I'll try."

"Good. Then you can put on the chip," he says, handing you another green-striped chip. Then he adds, "In case you want to try the reverse—having your bodily processes slow down —here's a red-striped chip."

Turn to page 51.

Strolling back home, you think about your situation. If you weren't speeded up, it would have taken you about four times as long to run the hundred meters—not even good enough to make the school track team. But now you can be a world-class star. If you trained a little, you could probably break every record in the book! Companies would pay you millions to advertise their products!

You start to let out a whoop of joy, but it dies in your throat. Something seems wrong about having time pass so fast for you and not for anyone else. And you don't like having to slow down your motions all the time so people won't think you're weird. By the time you go to bed that night, you're confused, wondering what to do.

After you've gone to sleep, you dream that the dream you're having now is reality, and what happened during the day was all just a dream!

When you wake up, you're more confused than ever.

If you decide to keep the chip on awhile longer, turn to page 46.

If you decide to take the chip off and return to normal speed, turn to page 36.

You reach in your pocket and pull out the green-striped chip. Wolfie doesn't quite see you do this, but he notices your quick motion.

"What are you doing, kid?" he barks.

You palm the chip. He hasn't seen it, but he's still suspicious. "Only way to keep you out of trouble is to tie you up." He pulls out some rope, and with the technique of a professional he whips it around your wrists and knots it. Then he ties your ankles the same way.

At that moment Jason stops at a traffic light. While Wolfie pulls the knot tightly around your ankles, Jason leaps out and starts running.

With a curse Wolfie vaults into the driver's seat and revs the engine. For a moment you're afraid he'll try to run Jason down, but Jason has already reached the sidewalk and is running into a building. Wolfie accelerates the van, then screeches around a corner and heads down a side street.

In the back, you struggle to loosen the rope around your wrists. You're thrown against the door as Wolfie makes a turn at high speed. Where is he taking you? You're a witness against him—he probably would like to get you out of the way.

Though you can't free your wrists, you're able to move your fingers. And you still have the green-striped chip clutched in your palm. It takes you a quick moment to pull off the protective tape and stick the chip behind your ear.

Turn to page 47.

During the week you take out the chips and look at them several times, but you avoid trying them out. The following Saturday you return to the lab in hopes that Dr. Telos will have other work for you.

"I didn't try on either of the chips," you say when you see him.

"Just as well," he says. "I decided I should have tried them out on myself first, so that's what I've been doing."

You're shocked. "Why did you try to get me to take them without first testing them on yourself?"

"That's a fair question," he says. "The answer is that my neurons aren't as young, healthy, and flexible as they are in a kid your age. At my age there's some risk that I wouldn't be able to reverse the effects, particularly with the green-striped chips, and that's what I'm noticing." Even as he's talking, Dr. Telos is making fast, jerky movements. He begins to look pale.

"What's the matter?" you ask.

Turn to page 78.

You're amazed to hear this, but you're too caught up in your own life to let it worry you. You quickly become known as the best athlete in your school. You can win every track race that comes along. In football, once you get the ball you can run around everyone in your way, scoring anytime you want. And in baseball, you soon learn that you have an advantage you hadn't even thought of—whether the pitcher is throwing a fast or a curve ball at you, it seems to be coming at only quarter speed. It's easy to keep your eye on it until it reaches the plate. By that time you're in midswing, connecting for a solid hit. No one can strike you out. And unless you hit a line drive that's caught, your speed always gives you an extra base or two. Quite often you make an inside-the-park home run out of what would normally be a single.

Soon you're getting a lot of offers to join professional teams. Your fame grows and grows. Within a couple of years, you've been on the covers of dozens of magazines—you've become more famous than anyone. TV shows beg you for interviews. Money pours in.

It's hard to think clearly when so much is happening. Still, you can't help but enjoy it. Life couldn't be better, you think.

Turn to page 116.

You pull off the chip, and just as Dr. Telos promised, your neural functions quickly return to normal.

When you return to the lab the following Saturday, Jason lets you in and shows you into the lab.

You're shocked to see Dr. Telos sitting rigidly on the chair in the Reality Machine. You call to him. He doesn't respond—he seems absolutely paralyzed. He doesn't even seem to be breathing!

"I don't like the looks of this," Jason says.

You feel the same way. You watch Dr. Telos intently. In a few seconds you notice an extremely slow movement of his head. After about half a minute more, his head has turned about an inch toward you and Jason.

Go on to the next page.

At that moment a recording begins playing—it's Dr. Telos's voice:

I have decided to visit the future. I am wearing two red-striped chips at once. My neural movements have probably slowed down to one one-hundredth of my normal speed. This means that by the time I think it's tomorrow, a hundred days will have passed. And by the time I think a year has passed, really a hundred years will have passed. Then I will be able to see life as it is a hundred years from now.

When the message ends, Jason reaches into the cabinet and pulls out a blood pressure monitor. He wraps a cloth around Dr. Telos's arm and takes a reading.

Turn to page 53.

"Geronimo!" You're out of the plane.

It races on overhead. You're in free-fall beneath it, twirling through the air.

The wind slows you. The plane races on. What a thrill!

You pull the rip cord. *Suppose the parachute doesn't open?*

It's not opening! You're still in free-fall, accelerating every second!

You pull the cord again. Still nothing!

You stare at the ground coming up at you— faster, faster, faster.

If only the parachute would open!

Instantly, a golden silken canopy flares out above you. You land, smiling, in a field of daisies.

Turn to page 118.

"I don't want any chips interacting with my brain," you tell Dr. Telos.

"I know it sounds dangerous," he says, "but it's really not. Anyway, come back next Saturday —I'll probably have some testing for you to do at level one. Meanwhile, take along one of each of these, in case you change your mind and decide to try one during the week." He hands you a green-striped chip and a red-striped one. You put them in your pocket.

Turn to page 33.

The next morning Dr. Telos visits you in your hospital room. "I'm sure glad you're okay," he says. "You're a hero. I'm leaving an envelope here for you. It's a check for the time you put in, plus a large bonus for being a hero."

"Thanks, Dr. Telos," you say. "I guess you went through a harrowing time yourself."

"Yes—it took a while for me to recover, I was so speeded up," he says. "I think from now on I'm going to stick to level one!"

The End

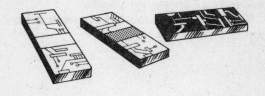

42

"Who are you?" Jason demands.

"Call me Wolfie," the intruder says with a snickering grin. He's short but powerfully built. A professional tough guy, you think.

"Take us back to the lab, Dr. Telos." Wolfie's tone is a dull monotone, but there's no doubting his meaning.

"I'm *not* Dr. Telos," Jason says.

"Sure," Wolfie says. "And I'm not holding a gun in my hand." To emphasize his point he jabs the muzzle into Jason's neck. Jason winces. He pulls a U-turn and heads the van back toward the lab.

You turn to face Wolfie. "Look, he's *not* Dr. Telos. Have him stop and show you his driver's license. You can see for yourself."

"Shut up, kid." A jab to your neck makes his point.

Turn to page 104.

Wolfie, knocked out for the moment, begins to stir. You waste no time getting his gun. You hold it on him while Jason calls the police.

While you're waiting for them to come, Jason drawls, "You can take that time chip off now if you want."

"Thanks. I'll probably take it off in a couple of days," you reply. "First I'm going to have a little fun."

The End

"I'll try it," you say.

"Good—you're a true pioneer!" Dr. Telos hands you one of the black chips. "This is a SUPER SPACE chip, programmed by the Reality Machine. Just pull off the tape and press it firmly behind your ear." You follow his instructions but don't notice any effect.

"What happens next?" you ask.

"This is the most fantastic part of it. Whenever you imagine something—like flying an airplane, for example—it will seem as if that's exactly what you're doing."

"That's wild," you say. "But suppose I start imagining something horrible?"

"You can just stop yourself," he says in a reassuring tone. "If your will is strong enough, then what you want to happen *will* happen."

This talk makes your head spin.

Dr. Telos rests a hand on your shoulder and looks you in the eye. "Look, you performed beautifully on level one. I'm confident you can handle level two."

"Shall I start now?"

"Sure, if you want," he says. "Or if you wish, you can try it out at home. Since the Reality Machine has already programmed the chip, you don't have to stay here."

If you decide to stay at the laboratory, turn to page 69.

If you decide to go home, turn to page 96.

46

You decide to keep the chip on and see what happens. Beginning the next day at school, you start trying to make all the teams, being careful not to show all your superhuman abilities at once, but just upping them gradually, as if you're getting better and better by training.

The next Saturday comes so fast that you forget all about Dr. Telos and your appointment. When you remember in the middle of the following week, you try to reach him on the phone. Jason answers and informs you that Dr. Telos has moved to a cabin in the wilderness and may not be back for many years, if ever. He tells you that Dr. Telos wants to concentrate on his TIME REALITY experiments—to prolong time for himself so that he can live much longer and observe the future. When he put on the red-striped chip, he slowed down so much that he couldn't do anything fast enough to live in civilization. He couldn't even cross the street before the light changed twice. So he decided the only safe place for himself was the wilderness.

Turn to page 34.

The next second the van pulls into a driveway. It swings around behind a large brick house before coming to a halt.

Wolfie drags you out, carries you into the house, and drops you on the kitchen floor. Meanwhile, you've speeded up. You can't get over how slowly he moves. If only you weren't tied up, you could easily get away.

Wolfie lifts the phone on the kitchen table and slowly dials a number. You hear him talking.

"You coming over, boss? . . . No, don't worry—they can't cause trouble. . . . Okay, see you in a few minutes." He looks around at you. "You might as well know, kid, when the boss gets here we're going to kill you."

This doesn't sound like idle talk. You're speeded up, and you've got a few minutes to do something. But tied up like this, what can you do?

Your ankles are tied, but you *could* stand up and then hop. You can probably hop faster than Wolfie can run! He might shoot at you, but you could probably dodge his bullets. Maybe.

You can't be sure until you try it.

Wolfie slowly turns away and opens the refrigerator, looking for food or drink. Should you make a break now or wait for a better chance?

*If you try to make a getaway,
turn to page 20.*

*If you wait for a better chance,
turn to page 56.*

At that moment you hear a siren—a police car coming down the street. Wolfie is reloading his gun. The driver of the pickup accelerates, leaving you exposed again. Just in time the cop car stops between you and Wolfie. You duck. The cop and Wolfie exchange shots.

Another cop car, coming from the other direction, finally comes to a halt. An officer leaps out in slow motion. Sitting in the car is Jason!

The firing has stopped. Over the hood of the police car you see why. Wolfie is stretched out on the pavement—the first cop got him.

More cops arrive. One of them cuts your ropes and takes you to the hospital. On the way you pull the chip off from behind your ear. To your relief you notice everything is speeding up, a sign that *your* time is leveling off to a normal pace.

You have bled quite a bit, and your thigh hurts a lot, but no serious damage has been done. The doctors tell you you'll be able to go home in a couple of days.

Turn to page 41.

50

"Thank you, Jason," Dr. Telos says.

Jason nods and leaves.

"You've seen this kind of dog before?" Dr. Telos asks.

"I'm not sure," you say. "They're very fast, aren't they? They race them at the dog track."

"Right. Greyhounds are faster than any other dog. But I don't race him at the track. He has more important work to do."

"He seems like a nice dog," you say, giving Merc a pat. "But I don't see what this has to do with affecting time."

The scientist smiles. "You'll see." He points at the chair. "Just sit in the Reality Machine and put on the gloves and headgear."

You follow his instructions, thinking there must be something extra to this game, and wondering what the dog has to do with it.

After putting on the helmet, you find that your field of vision is pitch-black for a moment. Then it lights up. A sign flashes in front of your eyes. It says, SUPER TIME—LEVEL ONE.

The sign fades. Then, to your surprise, the scene changes back to exactly what you saw a few moments ago—the big room with the green carpet, Dr. Telos a few feet away, Merc sitting at his feet.

"All set?" Dr. Telos asks. He leans over and presses a button on your armrest.

"I think so," you say. "But everything looks just the way it did before."

Turn to page 101.

You pocket the red-striped chip and put the green-striped one behind your ear. Once again, everything seems to have slowed down, as if time were passing faster for you than for the rest of the world. Watching Dr. Telos is like watching a film running in slow motion. Merc gets up and stretches, but so gradually it's almost comical. Even the second hand on the wall clock rotates at a snail's pace.

In contrast, you still move at normal speed—or so you think. According to Dr. Telos, all your movements are four times as fast as they normally would be.

"I think I'm ready," you say.

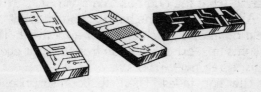

Turn to page 59.

"How is it?" you ask anxiously.

Jason shakes his head. "Too low. Very dangerous." With two swift motions, he rips first one and then the other chip from behind Dr. Telos's ear. The scientist stirs. He glances around, his head moving at normal speed again.

Jason explains to him what happened.

Dr. Telos gets up and walks unsteadily in a little circle. Then he wipes his brow. "Thank you, Jason," he says. "I'm disappointed not to have carried out my experiment but glad to still be alive."

"If you want to go into the future, you'd better do so more gradually," you comment.

"Yes, you're right—with only one red-striped chip this time," the scientist replies. "Would you like to come along?"

For a second you're tempted to put on a red-striped chip so that you too can visit the future. Then, as you think about it, you realize how much you would miss your family and friends. Living life at regular speed is adventuresome enough.

The End

54

You're alone again. For the first time you notice the peace and quiet of the woods, the calls of birds, and the buzzing of insects, though they are slowed to a drone. You reach down and try to untie the rope around your ankles but can't get it loose.

You rest a minute, trying to think what to do. You're still holding Wolfie's gun. You aim it at the ropes binding your ankles, then hesitate. If you don't hold the gun at precisely the right angle you could shoot yourself in the foot. Alone, deep in the woods, such an injury could be fatal.

If you try to sever the rope by firing at it, turn to page 115.

If you decide that firing is too risky, turn to page 95.

What's happened? Your spacecraft seems to be parked in an ordinary room! Of course, of course! You're not in a spacecraft, you're only in the Reality Machine!

Your clothes are drenched with sweat. What you've been through seemed so real.

"Welcome back to Earth. How are you feeling?" Dr. Telos helps you pull off your gloves and headgear.

You're still too shocked to speak.

"Are you all right?"

"Yes, sure." Wobbling a bit, you climb out of the machine.

Dr. Telos and Don Elman are both standing nearby, grinning. "You look like a sailor who's been at sea for a year and just set foot on dry land," Elman says. "But you were cool—terrific!"

"That was really something," you say.

Turn to page 108.

56

You decide to wait for a better chance. The boss, a square-faced, sallow man with puffy eyelids, arrives a few minutes later. He's in a fancy-looking striped suit. His shoes gleam as if they've just been polished.

"How do you want to do it, boss?" Wolfie asks.

The boss glances at you. "Take the kid deep in the woods and—you know what to do next, don't you, Wolfie?" he drawls.

Wolfie makes a noise halfway between a laugh and a snarl. "Sure, boss."

They can only move in slow motion compared to you, but you don't dare even twitch for fear of giving yourself away. The two of them pick you up and stuff you into the trunk of the boss's car. The lid slams down. Blackness envelops you.

A few moments later the car starts up. You're so scared you can hardly think straight, but you know you've got to do something fast.

You grope around the floor of the trunk. In one corner is a metal box. You manage to snap it open and feel inside. It's a tool kit. If only there's a knife in it.

You don't find a knife, but you do find a pair of wire cutters. Working with your fingers, you manage to position the jaws around the rope binding your wrist.

Getting them to cut isn't so easy. You hold the tool in place with your feet, but you can't bring enough pressure to bear on the jaws.

Turn to page 84.

You duck out of sight and crouch, listening. You hear a door creak, then voices and footsteps.

You wonder if they will pick up your trail.

Wolfie and the boss are arguing. You can't hear their words, but it's obvious they don't agree on what to do next. You're practically holding your breath, afraid that they'll hear your slightest movement.

The car doors slam, the engine starts up. You peek out and see them driving back down the road. They've given up! A thrill goes through you, but then you think again about how hungry and thirsty you are. You probably can't make it out of the woods, but you've got to try. You start hopping, but after a while you give up—it's just too tiring.

Turn to page 68.

Slowly he laughs. Very slowly he says, "Good . . . luck . . . then. . . . See . . . you . . . next . . . Saturday."

You thought you were ready, but when you walk out of the building this new reality is still a shock! People, cars—everything—seem to be moving much too slowly. You practice pacing yourself, so you won't look speeded up.

When you get home late that afternoon, you're eager to tell your family about what's happened, but you're worried it will upset them. Best not to mention it for now, you think.

You're not completely successful. Your mom notices that your movements seem jerky. You tell her everything's okay—you're feeling fine. The next day, Sunday, you work even harder at slowing your motions down, and after a while it begins to come naturally.

Turn to page 8.

You fire a laser blast and shield your eyes as the meteorite transforms into a fiery burst of light. Out of it fly thousands of shards and splinters—deadly missiles traveling at incredible speed.

You whip the steering yoke hard over. The spacecraft swerves, avoiding the fragments headed toward you, but turning into the path of others!

Words flash on the screen: COLLISION IN TEN SECONDS, NINE, EIGHT, SEVEN . . .

Desperately, you try a new evasion. The same thing happens. Now the nearest fragments are three seconds away, two, one— You realize you're finished, doomed!

"No!" you scream. You're passing out, yet you're still screaming. *"No! No! No! No!"*

"There, there—everything's all right."

You turn toward the voice and see a woman in a white coat standing beside you.

"I'm not dead? But I must be—" You realize that you can't be dead, you're lying in a bed.

"I'm Dr. Gerster," the woman says. "You're alive, and you're going to be all right."

You shudder as you remember the meteor fragments bearing down on you. You close your eyes, and your hands fly up, as if trying to shield yourself.

"Open your eyes. It's okay."

Turn to page 89.

You ignore him as you spot his holster, a forty-five bulging out of it. With lightning speed, you grab the gun, at the same time wrenching yourself loose. Wolfie loses his grip on you as well as his balance. You both fall to the ground.

Wolfie, surprised at how quickly you've plummeted to the ground, regains his footing. You're on your back, but you're aiming the gun right at him.

"Freeze!"

He stops short. "Hey, you must have one of those chips. Look, kid, put that gun down—we can work together."

"You didn't trust me, Wolfie, and I don't trust you," you say. "Now cut the rope on my ankles. One false move and you're dead, man!" The words sound good, but your voice is trembling. You don't like this situation one bit. Until your ankles are free, there's always a chance Wolfie can get the best of you.

"Sure, kid, I'll cut you free. I have a knife in the car." He starts toward the car. Even though he's moving in slow motion, you don't like to let him out of your line of fire. Suppose he's getting another gun?

"Stop!" you yell.

Turn to page 28.

You shoot at the tire and hit the mark. The air rushes out with a satisfying hiss.

Wolfie slowly gets out of the car. You train your weapon on him. Slowly he pulls a gun.

"Drop that!" you yell.

But he keeps walking toward you, one lingering step at a time. "There were only five bullets in the chamber, kid, and you've used them all."

You can see his finger slowly squeezing the trigger. You try to hop to your feet but not quite quickly enough. You duck the first bullet and try to duck the second one, but it hits your shoulder. You feel a stab of pain. Wolfie keeps coming, getting closer all the time, giving you less chance to see the bullets coming. There's no other choice. You take aim and squeeze the trigger.

Click.

Wolfie wasn't bluffing. Your gun is empty. His isn't.

The End

Something tells you to hold fire and wait to see what Wolfie does next.

The car starts backing up, coming right at you. He's trying to run you down!

With tremendous speed you pull yourself up and hop three steps to the left, positioning yourself behind a small tree. The car swerves and bashes into the tree, but you dodge free in time.

Wolfie leans out the window and aims another gun at you. You hop back several steps more. He fires.

You see the bullet coming and duck in time to miss it. Then you crouch, taking aim. With an oath, Wolfie ducks back into the car. The engine revs up. The car accelerates, this time in forward gear. You watch anxiously until it finally passes out of sight around a bend.

Turn to page 54.

"That was great. But if that was only level one, I don't think level two is for me," you say.

Dr. Telos frowns. He rubs his chin. "I'm sorry you don't want to try it, but I guess I can't blame you. Jason will pay you for your work on your way out."

"Thanks, sir—it was fun."

"I'm glad you enjoyed it," Telos says. "Would you like to come again next Saturday? I'll show you our new game, SUPER BASEBALL."

"Sure—I'll see you then. Same time?"

"Same time."

Turn to page 13.

You grit your teeth and try to ignore the aliens crawling over you. Slimy tentacles explore your shoulder and arms. One curls around your neck. The horror of their cold, clammy tissue is almost too much to bear. You're filled with a sense of foreboding that more will come, that there will be no end to them, that they will cover your entire body, wrapping you up like a bound mummy.

Then, to your relief, one, then another, and another, and finally every one of the loathsome creatures drops off and disappears. You wipe your brow and sigh with relief.

Everything goes black.

Turn to page 55.

You rest for a few minutes, then realize you have no alternative. You can't give up! You've got to make it!

Hop, hop . . . You miss your footing and fall hard on the sharp edge of a large rock.

Looking down, you see that the edge of rock has sliced through your jeans and scraped your skin. You're bleeding a little, and it hurts.

You sink down onto the ground. Why, after everything else, did you have to fall on a sharp rock?

A sharp rock! You were so tired you didn't realize your luck! You sit next to the rock and swing your legs over it, then rub the sharp edge against the ropes binding your ankles. In a few minutes you're free—and up on your feet, heading down the trail.

You're nearly exhausted, but you can still move fast. You reach the main road in no time and flag down a passing truck. The driver agrees to drop you off at the police station.

Along the way, you wonder whether you should stay speeded up or rip off the chip and get back to a normal time flow. Right now, you're so happy to be rescued that either way seems great.

The End

"I think I'll just stay here, Dr. Telos," you say. "I don't want my family seeing me until I know how this affects me."

"That's just fine. I suggest you sit on the couch in the lounge by the reception room, close your eyes, and relax. Then you'll be setting out on an adventure that *you* create."

Dr. Telos shows you into the lounge. You sit on the couch, lean back, and close your eyes.

Nothing happens.

Could this all be a failure? Maybe Dr. Telos did something wrong.

You glance at your watch—ten minutes must have gone by. Still nothing. Dr. Telos is gone. You wish he were here—you'd ask him why nothing's happened.

Suddenly he appears before you. "Nothing working yet?" he asks. "Be patient." Just as suddenly he's gone again!

How could he do that? Appearing and disappearing like that—like a magician. Then you realize that he didn't appear and disappear—he only seemed to! The vision you saw was created by your own brain, along with those chips!

It's as if anything you imagine can happen! It's scary, but it could be fun. What can you think of next? What do you really want to imagine?

Turn to page 100.

70

You chase after him out of the building. A blurry movement flashes by. It's Dr. Telos running, moving faster than the cars on the street. He must have figured that he could run to the hospital faster than an ambulance could take him.

Jason has come out and is standing next to you.

"He's already out of sight around the block," you say.

"I'd better drive to the hospital," Jason says. "We'll take the company van." He points to a van parked nearby with the name REALITY UNLIMITED painted in gold letters on the side.

You think of the chips in your pocket. Dr. Telos said the red-striped ones slow down neural speed. "I'd better come along," you tell Jason. "One of these chips might be an antidote for him."

"Come on, then," Jason says. He drives as fast as he can through the dense traffic. You've gone about two blocks and are stopped at a light when a man rushes up and forces his way into the back of the van. Jason yells angrily but is cut short when the man flashes a gun.

Turn to page 42.

You decide not to put on the chip. A few minutes later Jason pulls the van up to the offices of Reality Unlimited.

Wolfie snarls, "Get out."

You and Jason get out of the car. Wolfie, covering you with his gun, marches you into the building.

There's no one at the reception desk. Wolfie forces Jason to unlock the door to the lab. Inside you're met by Merc, who barks sharply at the intruder. Wolfie gives the animal only a sidelong glance—Merc is obviously not a guard dog.

Wolfie levels his gun at Jason. "Okay, where are the time chips?"

"Please don't point that at me. I'll get them." Jason's voice is shaking. He opens a cabinet and takes out the dish with the red-striped chips and the dish with the green-striped chips. He empties the dishes out onto a table.

"What's the difference between these?" Wolfie says.

"If you put a red-striped chip on your skin behind your ear it will speed you up. If you put on a green-striped chip it will slow you down." Jason is lying, hoping that Wolfie will attach a red-striped chip and slow down so much that Jason can take the gun away. But Wolfie looks at him shrewdly.

Go on to the next page.

"You're lying, aren't you?"

Jason looks offended. "I'm *not* lying," he says. "I'm not that brave."

For a second Wolfie seems convinced, but then he scowls. "Okay, if you're not lying, take one of the red-striped ones and put it on."

"Sure," Jason says. He picks up one of the red-striped chips, tears off the adhesive, and is about to put it on when Wolfie slaps his hand aside, sending the chip spinning onto the floor.

Turn to page 103.

"See, I don't have it," Jason says, very slowly.

Wolfie looks back at the dog, who is trying to shake the chip off. Finally it pops off onto the rug.

Wolfie glances at you, but you're sitting still. He brandishes his gun at Jason. "This time you're going to put it on right. I'll kill you before I ask you again!"

Jason is shaking, perhaps with fear, but you're pretty sure he's acting, stalling for time. Wolfie hands him another red-striped chip. "Do it. Now!"

Jason calls Merc over and again puts the chip on the inside of the dog's ear. This time the chip stays on long enough so that when Merc tries shaking it off, you can hardly tell he's moving. He's in slower motion than Wolfie and Jason!

Wolfie lets out a long laugh.

"So, the red-striped ones slow you down! That means the green-striped ones speed you up!"

He reaches over and grabs a green-striped chip, waving it triumphantly at Jason and then at you. "There's going to be a lot of fun when I'm speeded up, and I don't want anyone to spoil it. Both of you—facedown on the floor. Now!"

"You don't need to shoot us!" Jason protests.

"That's for me to decide," Wolfie says. "Now lie down, or you'll die a very quick death."

Turn to page 24.

You return to the Reality Machine and follow his instructions. Your vision blurs and then clears again. You blink as you see Merc standing next to Dr. Telos, wagging his tail so slowly that you can't believe it. All his other movements are slowed down as well, and Dr. Telos's too, as the scientist reaches over to pat the dog.

"This is amazing," you say as you gesture with your hands. They move at normal speed, unlike the smile forming with incredible slowness on Dr. Telos's face.

"As the old saying goes," he says, "you ain't seen nothing yet." Even Dr. Telos's speech seems slow. And in equally slow motion, he takes a rubber ball out of the cabinet. He begins moving it up behind his shoulder as if he's going to throw it. Gradually Merc raises his head, following it with his eyes.

"Now you'll see if you can outrace a greyhound," Dr. Telos says slowly. "When I throw the ball, I want you to get it before Merc does."

"You mean I should actually run after it?"

"Sure. Forget you're wearing a special helmet and gloves. Just run for the ball." In absurdly slow motion the scientist continues to rear back his arm. Merc, seeing what's happening, slowly begins to tense, getting ready to run. Dr. Telos's arm moves forward, and a couple of seconds later his fingers begin to open. You watch the ball rolling along the underside of his fingers.

Turn to page 25.

You rush Wolfie, attempting to knock the gun out of his hand. In the few steps it takes to reach him, you watch as a look of surprise slowly forms on his face. At the same time he's swinging his gun to take aim at you. Even though you're quicker, he'll have it aimed at you before you can grab the muzzle.

You duck. A bullet whistles by your ear. You grab the muzzle of his gun. It's hot from having just been fired, and you have to let go.

Wolfie grabs for you with his free hand. You duck out of his reach. Again he aims the gun at you and you dodge another bullet.

Immediately you feel the weight of his other arm bearing down.

You drop into a crouch to shake him off, then hesitate—thinking how you've got to keep Wolfie from pointing his gun at you and at the same time keep out of his reach.

That moment of hesitation costs you your speed advantage. Wolfie has his burly arm around your neck. He squeezes mercilessly. Then you hear a dull thump. Wolfie's arm goes limp. A second later he slumps to the floor. Jason is standing behind him, a big grin on his face. In his hands is the computer he just brought down on Wolfie's head.

Turn to page 44.

"I was wearing the green-striped chip. I took it off, but I'm still programmed by it!" His head begins to jerk violently.

"Sir, I think maybe you should see a doctor."

"You're right." You see the blur of his hand moving while he picks up the phone. "Jason— get me an ambulance. I think I'm going into convulsions." His speech is now speeded up so much you can barely understand him.

There's another blur—and Dr. Telos is out the door. It's astonishing—his motions have accelerated so much that your eyes can hardly follow him!

Turn to page 70.

"Everything's checked out," Telos says. "From now on your experience won't be happening in the outer world but in your own head. Remember not to panic or be frightened. Whatever happens to you isn't *really* happening, it's just an illusion."

A sign flashes in front of your eyes. It says SUPER SPACE—LEVEL ONE. The sign fades. Then the scene is exactly as you saw it before—

"Nothing's happening yet," you say.

Dr. Telos nods. "That's because the computer is programmed to show the world just as you would see it if you weren't hooked up to it. Everything, except . . . look around."

Turn to page 93.

"I'll choose SUPER SPACE," you say.

"Very good." Dr. Telos fiddles with the controls of the Reality Machine a moment, then slips a huge disc into one of the hard drives.

"Ready," he announces in a satisfied tone. "Okay, sit in the chair. While you put on the gloves and helmet, I'm going to call someone in."

When you're rigged up, things look just as they did before.

Dr. Telos is hanging up the telephone. "We'll get started in a moment," he says.

Another man, unusually short and dressed in a lab coat like Dr. Telos, comes into the room.

Dr. Telos beckons him over. "This is Don Elman, our marketing manager."

Elman smiles at you from under his jaunty handlebar mustache. "We think the Reality Machine is going to blow the socks off the entertainment industry," he says.

"You mean everyone will be playing it?"

"More than that," Elman says. "It's going to change people's lives. With this machine, people can get the same experience they would traveling to distant countries. Whatever appeals to you—whether it's playing basketball, car racing, skiing in the Alps, diving for buried treasure—you name it—it will be just as much fun, and maybe more."

"This has got to be something big!" you say.

Turn to page 91.

At that moment one of them drops onto your head. You feel its tentacle dragging over your left ear. Another one slides its slimy body across your neck. The tentacles of yet another grip your shoulder like the fingers of a cold, clammy hand. You reach up to pull it off, but then stop short, remembering the warning—"will attack when angry."

Maybe you should leave the thing alone. But what if the warning is wrong? You can't just let them bite you. What if they're poisonous?

*If you try to pull the aliens off,
turn to page 94.*

*If you leave them alone,
turn to page 67.*

You hesitate, then decide to think of a way to get Jason to distract Wolfie. You've got to think fast, though, before Wolfie puts on the chip he's holding. You catch Jason's eye. To give him a signal, you move your arm so fast that anyone not speeded up would see only a blur of light.

Jason lets out a cry and clutches his throat. For a moment you think he's in pain, then you realize that he's supplying the distraction you wanted.

You charge Wolfie, faster than the wind. He barely senses your approach. You knock the gun out of his hand with a terrific kick. It sails in slow motion across the room. You catch it before it hits the ground, whirl, and yell, *"Freeze!"*

Wolfie, openmouthed, obeys.

"Great . . . going!" Jason says slowly.

"Same goes for you," you reply.

While you keep an eye on Wolfie, Jason puts a call in to the police. Waiting for them to come, you try to decide what to do next with your superhuman speed. You smile, thinking about the Olympic medals you could win.

The End

You try to relax, remembering that the car is only poking along. You have extra time to work carefully, though the suspension of time is nerve-racking.

You shift position and brace one handle of the wire cutters against the wall of the trunk, then press your foot against the other handle. The jaws cut two strands of the rope and half the remaining one. You're almost free, but then you realize the car has crawled to a stop. The engine dies. You hear the driver's door open.

Like a trapped animal, you hold your wrists to your mouth and gnaw at the frayed rope. The lid of the trunk lifts slowly up. You keep gnawing, and you feel your wrists pull apart—you've cut the rope!

You bring your wrists back together so Wolfie won't notice that they're free. Then you feel his hands grabbing under your shoulders, lifting you out. Blinking in the bright light, you see that he's parked the car on a dirt road. Dense woods surround you.

"You've got about ten feet to travel, kid," Wolfie says. "Just over to these bushes."

He gets another hand under your knees. "Not even going to thrash around? I was hoping for a little fight in you."

Turn to page 62.

"Ten, nine, eight . . ."

You tighten your seat belt and hold on to the wheel.

". . . four, three, two, one, LAUNCH!"

The rocket takes off with tremendous acceleration. You're thrown back against your seat. The nose tilts. In a few seconds you're flying straight up, through the clouds into the deep blue sky.

"Launch successful," the voice announces.

But a red warning light is blinking. Data flashes on the screen. The voice announces: "Meteorite on collision course. Present bearing three twenty-seven, eight miles above you."

You see a small, irregular shape approaching on the screen.

"Meteorite on collision course," the voice says.

Clutching the steering yoke, you study the instruments, wondering what you can do.

The blue sky ahead darkens into black. You've risen above the stratosphere and are already in space. Below, half the Earth is shrouded in night. The other half is a swirling pattern of white clouds, green land, and blue water.

Turn to page 105.

86

Suddenly you explode out of the gate, snow flying in your eyes, racing down the almost vertical slope. Crouching, then striding to gain more speed, you hit a mogul and take to the air. You land firmly and accelerate again, plunging almost in free-fall down the mountain.

An even steeper dip looms ahead; then a tree comes at you. You're afraid you'll crash! You try to turn, but your legs slide out from under you, and you're whipped hard into the tree. *If only you hadn't crashed!*

Miraculously there's no pain! Miraculously you're on your feet again, skiing faster than ever, passing all your opponents, streaking across the finish line, doffing your hat to the crowd.

Turn to page 118.

"The adhesive side has tape protecting it," Dr. Telos says. "Don't pull it off until you're ready to put the chip against your skin—then save the tape for when you want to take the chip off."

"I don't know about this interaction stuff," you say. "It might not be good for my brain."

"It's harmless," Dr. Telos says firmly. "In any event the chips are used only for level two. For level one it's just gloves and the headset."

"That's no problem," you say. "I'm ready to begin—level one, I mean."

"Fine," Dr. Telos says. "Which shall it be then—SUPER TIME or SUPER SPACE?"

If you choose SUPER TIME, *turn to page 17.*

If you choose SUPER SPACE, *turn to page 80.*

You obey. The doctor is still standing there. She rests a hand gently on your shoulder.

"I know it was horrible, but it didn't happen. It didn't happen—you must keep that in mind."

"But it was so real—and that was only level one!"

She nods. "The reality wasn't in the danger of space travel but in the danger to your mind. If you'd spent much longer in that machine, you probably would have gone completely insane. As it is, I can assure you that you're going to be completely all right."

You sit up and look around the room. Sunlight is streaming through the window.

"Feeling better?" the doctor asks.

"A little better." You grin at her. She's writing something on a notepad.

"Are you going to give me a prescription, Doc?"

"Just one," she says. "Never, *never* play the Reality Machine again!"

The End

To evade the meteorite, you whip the steering yoke over. The craft turns sharply. The meteorite passes so close it takes your breath away. Then everything seems normal again—but only for an instant. A buzzer sounds, and a warning flashes on your computer screen: DANGER: CALIBRATE THRUSTERS.

Calibrate thrusters? What does that mean? Your eyes scan the instrument panel as you try to figure out what to do.

You feel a wet sensation on the back of your neck and reach behind you. A pinch on your thumb makes you jerk your hand away. You glance around. Slimy, crablike creatures are crawling on the back of your seat. One of them has you by the ear!

You yell and yank it off.

Shaking, bleeding, you type a question in the computer:

"Crablike aliens in spacecraft. Analysis!"

An answer appears almost instantly on the screen. "Aliens probably of the aractopod type. Generally harmless but will attack when angry."

Turn to page 81.

"You'll soon get a chance to prove it for yourself," Dr. Telos says.

"You may get so caught up in it, you'll forget it's a game," Elman joins in.

"Just exactly how does it work?" you say.

"Don, you explain," Telos says to his colleague.

"Be glad to. SUPER SPACE is designed not just to simulate sights and hand movements, but to simulate your whole body—all your senses. For example, if you're taking a turn at high speed, you'll feel centrifugal force pressing your body toward the outside of the turn."

"You'll not only see your craft as it performs, you'll *feel* the pressure," Dr. Telos says. "You'll have to brace yourself to keep from leaning sideways."

"It won't be just virtual reality," Elman adds. "It will be reality itself."

"Well, I'd say that about level two but not this level," Dr. Telos says. "Anyway, shall I activate it?"

"Activate," you say.

You hear a pleasing musical tone. A green light flashes briefly on the panel before you.

Turn to page 79.

You glance around again and blink several times. Don Elman has suddenly grown about a foot. He was quite a bit shorter than Dr. Telos, and now suddenly he's much taller.

You blurt out, "Is that really you?"

Suddenly a straw hat appears on his head; then you notice that his mustache has disappeared and a beard is growing. Within a few seconds it's almost down to his chest!

"It *is* me, and no, I didn't just get a foot taller and grow a long beard. And I'm not wearing a straw hat." Even as he says this, he turns back to his normal size, the beard turns back into a mustache, and the straw hat disappears. He raises a forefinger. "This little practice demonstration is to show you that what happens in the Reality Machine is not really happening. If you believe otherwise, you might have a heart attack. Some pretty wild things are going to happen to you—but not really."

"Well, I'm ready," you say.

Dr. Telos pats your shoulder. "Good. Now, you'll soon be taking off on a mission to Mars. Just do your best in the situations that come up. The program only lasts half an hour or less. No matter what happens, it will soon be over."

Turn to page 16.

You peel off the tentacle gripping your shoulder, but almost instantly another one replaces it, then yet another slithers along beside it, pinching your skin. You manage to peel it back, but it is quickly replaced by two others! Panicked, you rip faster at the alien flesh. You scream—you feel you're going mad!

A blazing light blinds you; then everything goes black.

You sit in the dark quiet of your chair, breathing hard, trying to recover your senses. Slowly you remember—what just happened didn't happen—it was an illusion. You open your eyes. Dr. Telos is standing next to you, a worried look on his face. It's not surprising, if you look the way you feel—completely wiped out.

"How was it?" he asks. "Are you all right?"

"Yes, I'm all right," you say in a dull tone. "But you'll have to find someone else to test your games. I've had enough of machine-made reality. From now on I'm sticking with the real thing."

The End

You decide it's too risky to aim a bullet so close to your feet. But now what will you do? You're sure it must be a couple of miles to a well-traveled road. You can't hop that far. But how will anyone find you here?

You sit thinking, trying to keep a cool head. But instead of coming up with an idea, you just grow more worried. Are you going to starve? Or die of thirst? Suppose Wolfie comes back with the boss? You wouldn't want to have to fight both of them off. You'd better get out of sight, first thing. You start hopping off into the woods, looking for a place to hide.

After a few minutes you stop to rest. Suddenly you hear a car coming up the road. You hop behind a clump of hemlocks, hoping to find cover, then freeze as the car gradually comes into view. You can see it through a gap in the branches, and the boss and Wolfie are in it.

Turn to page 58.

On your way home you think about how upset your parents would be if they knew you were wearing an electronic chip that affected your sense of reality. You decide not to mention it, and not to begin imagining things. Everything is fine until you go to bed and your mind begins to wander. Thinking about a science program you saw starts you thinking about a space voyage to a new planet . . .

Your spacecraft has safely landed. You're stepping out onto a dreamlike landscape where the ground is covered with moss and huge fern trees rise all about you.

Aliens come forward to greet you. They look like apes, only they have scaly bodies and shining green eyes.

You walk up to the closest of them. "We come in peace from the planet Earth," you say.

Another alien comes at you. You try to run, but it seizes you in its mighty arms!

Screaming, you struggle to free yourself.

Turn to page 109.

"That's what *you* thought," your mother says. "And we thought you'd gone crazy. We were very worried, and we called the paramedics. When they arrived, you just went wild. They couldn't quiet you down. They had to give you an injection and take you to the hospital. The doctors couldn't figure out what was wrong with you until they found something pasted on the skin behind your ear. They took it off, and you stopped your babbling right away."

"Oh, yes—the chip from the Reality Machine." Your memory of everything that happened comes back to you, and you tell your mother the whole story.

"What a nightmare," she says. "I hope you'll never do anything like that again!"

"No way, Mom," you say, and you never meant anything more in your life.

The End

"That's something I never dreamed could happen."

"It could, and it *can*," he says. "And you can be the first to experience it. A great explorer, a pioneer in one of humankind's greatest adventures!"

Dr. Telos is a genius, and he seems to be completely sure of what he's doing. It's a very tempting offer. But dare you accept it?

If you dare to try level two, turn to page 45.

If you say, "No way!" turn to page 66.

Images race through your mind—skiing in the Olympics, diving for treasure, skydiving, landing a spacecraft on Mars!

Which do you want to do most?

If you want to ski in the Olympics, turn to page 86.

If you want to dive for treasure, turn to page 106.

If you want to skydive, turn to page 39.

If you want to land a spacecraft on Mars, turn to page 110.

"It's supposed to," he says. "That's the way this game begins. Are you right-handed or left-handed?"

You tell him.

"Okay—I asked because you'll notice a red lever set in the outside of each of your armrests. Right-handers only need to use the one on the right, and left-handers only need to use the one on the left. Move the lever forward to speed up time and back to slow it down. Understand?"

"I think so. How much does it speed up or slow down?"

"You'll get a feel for that when you play the game," he says. "Now you can unhook all your cables—you won't need them. Minicomputers in your helmet have copied the program for this game."

Turn to page 113.

"No you don't! If you *are* telling the truth, that would speed you up."

"But you asked me to," Jason says.

"That was to test you. Now I know you were telling the truth."

"Okay," Jason says. "Then you know which one to put on."

Wolfie glares at him, then at you, obviously uncertain what to do. Then his eyes light up. "The dog! I'll try it on the dog. Then I can be sure which chip does what."

He makes Jason call Merc over. "Okay, attach it to him," he orders Jason.

"He has too much hair—it won't stick," Jason says.

Wolfie pats the dog and turns up his ears. "Here—on the inside of his ear!"

Merc allows Jason to affix the chip to the tender skin on the underside of one of his ears.

Wolfie watches. "Is it on tight?"

"Yes," Jason says, withdrawing his hand.

Wolfie moves in on him. "Open your hand— you still got it in your hand!"

So far, you have only been able to watch. Now, while Wolfie is distracted, you have a chance to affix a green-striped chip behind your ear. Jason, facing you, has probably noticed, but not Wolfie. His eyes are on Jason, who is holding out his empty hand.

Turn to page 74.

In the few minutes it takes to get back to the lab, you try to think what to do. The thug must be after the chips from the Reality Machine. You shudder to think what crimes he could commit if he got them. He could rob banks and make his escape in a blur of light. In a shoot-out with the law, the cops wouldn't have a chance against him.

You wish you could do something, but you feel helpless with an armed man pointing a gun at your head. Except there *is* one thing you can do —put the green-striped chip behind your ear. With the speed it would give you, you could foil Wolfie and maybe save lives. But you've never tried the chip. And what if Wolfie notices?

If you decide to put on the green-striped chip, turn to page 32.

If you decide it's too risky, turn to page 72.

The meteorite is still approaching. Your eye rests on a panel with a knob labeled TARGET ACQUISITION. Next to it is a red button with the word FIRE under it.

You adjust the knobs until the target is in the cross hairs.

The object on the screen grows rapidly larger. You've got to act!

*If you try to destroy the meteorite,
turn to page 61.*

*If you try to evade it,
turn to page 90.*

106

Depth: 140 feet. Oxygen supply: eighteen minutes. Before you, half buried in sand, is the split hull of a Spanish galleon, its ancient timbers encrusted with sea moss and barnacles.

Brilliantly colored fish swim in and out of a gaping hole in its side—the result of a hurricane over four hundred years ago.

Shining your searchlight along the stern, you notice faint indentations. You scrape away the sea growth with your knife. Letter by letter the name of the ship is revealed: the *Santa Marquesa!*

You've found it! The vessel that sank with the royal jewels of the Incas aboard! You hurry toward the opening, eager to find the captain's quarters, where you've read the jewels were stowed.

You've been so excited you haven't thought about the danger. Now, as you prepare to enter the dark recesses of the ship, you pause. *Suppose a shark is lurking beneath the overhanging deck?*

One is! A great white, coming at you, its jaws open wide enough to swallow you whole!

Terror seizes you. The horror is beyond anything you'd ever imagined.

The great jaws close upon you. *If only you were stronger than a shark . . .*

You are! With superhuman strength, you pry its jaws apart, flip the shark over, and ascend triumphantly to the surface.

Turn to page 118.

Don Elman straps a band around your arm. "I want to take your blood pressure, just as they do with astronauts after space flight." He pumps a little black ball and consults the gauge. "Hmmm, good. You didn't panic. You handled stress well. You performed magnificently under extreme conditions. You'd make an excellent astronaut."

"Being an astronaut can't be any more real than the Reality Machine," you say.

Dr. Telos grins. "I'm glad you feel that way," he says. "And that was only level one! Are you ready for level two?"

"With those black electronic chips? It seems kind of spooky."

"If you want the game to stop, you just pull the chip off with your fingers," Telos says.

"Still, this sounds too wild for me," you say.

"Of course, the choice is up to you," he says, obviously disappointed. "But before you turn down this opportunity, consider that these chips are the wave of the future—the next great leap forward for human progress. People won't have to worry whether they are having good experiences. Everything they want will be obtainable just by wishing for it!"

Turn to page 99.

You wake up in a hospital bedroom. Your mom is standing by your bedside.

"Mom, what happened?"

"A lot," she says. "Last night, as you were about to go to bed, you came up to me and said, 'We come in peace from planet Earth.' I thought that was *very* strange. I called to your father, and when he came, you turned and started wrestling with him. You were shouting and yelling, making no sense at all."

"Oh, I remember—I was on some strange planet," you say.

Turn to page 98.

The red planet rises to meet you, and you marvel at its beauty in the stark light of the distant sun: towering volcanos that haven't stirred in a billion years; canyons of staggering depth, once sculpted by roaring water, now dry and devoid of life.

Your spacecraft descends toward the smooth plain. *If only there were life on this desolate planet!*

A strip of green comes into view. Trees, houses!

You alter course and settle in for a landing in the green strip, keeping an eye out for the Martian dust storms you've been warned about.

One's coming! A swirling red cloud blows off the plain. In seconds it envelops your craft. Everywhere, all you can see is dust, red dust, then darkness. . . .

CRASH!

Turn to page 118.

As you're talking on the phone, Dr. Telos swings his arms violently from back to front; then, relaxing his hands, he looks over your head and breaks into a broad grin. Once again he begins jogging around the room.

There must have been a patrol car cruising nearby, because the police are on the scene in less than a minute. Two officers rush into the lab, looking as if they expect resistance. They stop short and stand watching with bemused faces as Dr. Telos repeats his routine.

"I've seen a lot of nuts in my day," one of the officers says, "but this takes the cake."

"How long has he been like this?" the other asks you.

"Ever since I came in a few minutes ago," you say.

"Hey, you," the first cop yells at Dr. Telos.

But the scientist keeps looking away, swinging his hands back and forth.

"Just what does he think he's doing?" the other cop asks.

Dr. Telos suddenly swings his arms violently, then looks happily off into space, then starts jogging around another square.

At that moment you remember that Dr. Telos invited you over to try the new SUPER BASEBALL game. You realize what's happening.

"He thinks he's playing baseball, and that he's a home run king," you tell the cops. "Babe Ruth maybe. He's hitting one homer after another!"

Turn to page 21.

When you're unhooked, Dr. Telos instructs you: "Walk over and stand next to Merc."

You do as he says, surprised that you don't have to sit in the Reality Machine.

Standing next to Merc, you look over at Dr. Telos, who is grinning, obviously pleased with what he's about to show you.

"Do you think you can run faster than Merc?" he asks.

"Than a greyhound? Of course not," you say.

"Well, with the help of the Reality Machine, you'll be able to."

"How?"

"By slowing down time except for yourself. For example, move the lever back to slow down time by a factor of four."

Turn to page 75.

You aim, trying to keep your hand steady, and fire. The rope frays. The bullet smashes harmlessly into the dirt. You let out a sigh. A few threads are still holding, but by twisting the rope, pulling and tugging, you sever them too. You kick the ends off and stiffly stretch your feet, then bend over and rub the sore, bruised skin where the ropes held your ankles. Then you start jogging down the dirt road, anxious to get out of the woods as quickly as possible.

It's a mile and a half from where you are to a well-traveled road, but it takes you only a few minutes to cover the distance.

Once you reach the road, you try to flag down a car. Several pass by. Finally one pulls to a stop. It's Wolfie's!

A hail of bullets comes at you—and there's no place to hide.

The End

One day a few years later you're standing outside your mansion next to your Olympic-sized swimming pool when you happen to notice your reflection in the water. Strangely, you hardly recognize yourself. You run into the house, to one of your marble-tiled bathrooms, and study your face in the mirror. Suddenly you realize what's wrong. You look much older than you are. *What's going on? How could this happen?*

Slowly the answer comes to you: you've been able to increase the speed of your movements because your neural processes have been speeded up. But that means your rate of aging has speeded up as well. By the time you're twenty, you'll be middle-aged. By the time you're thirty, you'll have white hair!

Suddenly all your fame, all your riches, all your fantastic abilities seem worthless. It's very depressing.

You think back to the time you let Dr. Telos put the chip behind your ear. The chip has been there so long now, you've almost forgotten you can easily pull it off. But it's too late—it won't make you look younger. If only you could slow down time . . . You vaguely remember the red-striped chip Dr. Telos gave you. If you could just remember where it is . . .

The End

You're sitting on the couch, just as you were before, but now you're staring up at the ceiling, remembering vividly what you've just experienced—the most exciting, and also the most terrifying, moments of your life.

Dr. Telos is standing by you, a jubilant expression on his face. "I can see the Reality Machine worked. Congratulations!"

Still a little shaky from your ordeal, you try to pull the chip off from behind your ear. It won't come off!

Dr. Telos takes a close look. "The adhesive is not supposed to stick that hard," he says.

"Well, it did!" you practically shout.

"I can get it off," he says. "But it will hurt."

"Well, get it off anyway!"

He rips it off, with a bit of your skin. *"Ouch!"* you yell.

"Sorry about that," Dr. Telos says. "Jason, get some bandages and disinfectant!"

Still shaking, you get to your feet. The scientist smiles in a way that's meant to be friendly but seems in fact smug and self-satisfied.

"I'm sure that won't happen next time," he says.

"There's not going to be a next time," you say. "From now on I'm going to stick with SURREAL ACTION!"

The End

ABOUT THE AUTHOR

EDWARD PACKARD is a graduate of Princeton University and Columbia Law School. He developed the unique storytelling approach used in the Choose Your Own Adventure series while thinking up stories for his children, Caroline, Andrea, and Wells.

ABOUT THE ILLUSTRATOR

JUNE BRIGMAN has been drawing since she was old enough to hold a pencil. She studied art at the University of Georgia and Georgia State University, but her illustrations are based on real-life observation and skills she developed over a summer as a pastel portrait artist at Six Flags Over Georgia amusement park, when she was only sixteen. Shortly thereafter she discovered an interest in comic books, and by the time she was twenty-two she got her first job working for Marvel Comics, where she created the Power Pack series. Ms. Brigman currently lives and works in White Plains, New York.

FRENCH TOAST PROFILE

NAME: Brandon Scott

AGE: 11

HOBBY: Riding Roller Coasters.

FAVORITE BOOKS: Choose Your Own Adventure®

FAVORITE ACTIVITY: Bike racing.

FAVORITE MOVIE: Indiana Jones.

GOAL IN LIFE: Be the first to live on the moon.

CLOTHES: French Toast.

Clothes, footwear and accessories.
You don't eat 'em. You wear 'em.®

How you can become the star of the next French Toast Profile.